# NOT THIS TURKEY!

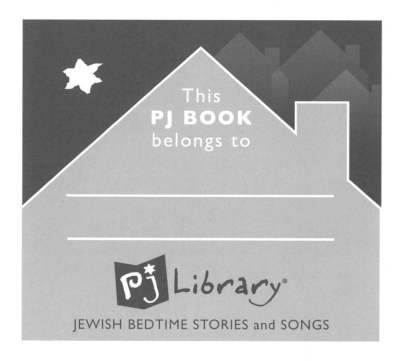

This
**PJ BOOK**
belongs to

_____

_____

**pj** Library®

JEWISH BEDTIME STORIES and SONGS

**JESSICA STEINBERG**

pictures by
**AMANDA PIKE**

Albert Whitman & Company
Chicago, Illinois

For the Silberklangs; Deborah Brodie; and Daniel,
my main Thanksgiving muse—JS

For Dave, my favorite and best—AP

Library of Congress Cataloging-in-Publication
data is on file with the publisher.

Text copyright © 2016 by Jessica Steinberg
Illustrations copyright © 2016 by Albert Whitman & Company
Pictures by Amanda Pike
Published in 2016 by Albert Whitman & Company
ISBN 978-0-8075-7912-1
Printed in China
10 9 8 7 6 5 4 3 2 1 WKT 22 21 20 19 18 17
Design by Jordan Kost

For more information about Albert Whitman & Company,
visit our website at www.albertwhitman.com.

101726.7K1/B1100/A6

When I was still a baby, my family moved to the United States.

We lived in a tenement house on 33 Debevoise Street in Williamsburg—me, Mama and Papa, and then my little brother, David, who was born in America.

Every morning after Papa walked me to school, he would take the train to Mr. Deutsch's pocketbook factory on the Lower East Side. He said that when the subway crossed over the Williamsburg Bridge, he could see all the way to the Empire State Building.

Papa said he sometimes missed Germany, but he also liked figuring out how things were done in America.

Like the morning Mrs. Deutsch told Papa to put his name down for the Thanksgiving raffle.

"What's a raffle?" Papa asked.

"Don't be such a greenhorn," said Mrs. Deutsch. "It's a Thanksgiving prize."

We had been living in New York for four years, but we had never celebrated Thanksgiving. Mama made stuffed cabbage and noodle kugel for our holidays.

But that day Papa said to Mrs. Deutsch, "Why not? New country, new celebrations."

It was almost closing time when Mr. Deutsch came out of his office and yelled, "Time for the raffle!"

"Feh, who cares?" said Mr. Schwartz. "That cheapskate Deutsch is probably giving away a sack of potatoes."

But Papa had a funny feeling in the pit of his stomach, like the way he felt when we got our visas to come to America.

Mr. Deutsch put his hand into the cardboard box and pulled out a piece of paper.

"And the winner is," announced Mr. Deutsch, "Baruch Silberklang!"

Everyone clapped. Papa couldn't believe it. He'd won.

"Mazel tov, Mr. Silberklang!" called Mr. Deutsch.
"You can celebrate Thanksgiving this year."

Mrs. Deutsch came out of the office, lugging a
huge turkey behind her.

"Here you go, Silberklang," said Mr. Deutsch. "Your very own turkey."

Papa looked at the turkey. It was bigger than any chicken Mama had ever made.

"How will you get it home?" asked Mr. Schwartz.

"The J train," Papa sighed. "How else?"

It was a long walk to the subway. Papa was never so glad to see the train pull into the station.

But it wasn't so easy once he got on. The turkey was noisy.

When they reached the Flushing Avenue stop, Papa took the turkey out of the box and held on to its rope. But as soon as he stepped off the train, a big gust of wind blew off his fedora.

Papa ran after his hat, and the turkey ran in the other direction.

"Come back here!" yelled Papa.

Papa ran after the turkey and grabbed the rope. Then he ran after his hat and caught it with his shoe.

Finally, holding on tightly to his hat, Papa and the turkey walked down the stairs to the street.

All the neighbors stopped to stare at Papa and his turkey when he walked down our street.

"Whatcha got there, Mr. Silberklang?" asked Mrs. Caporimo.

Papa just smiled at her and pulled the turkey up the stairs to the fourth floor, where we lived.

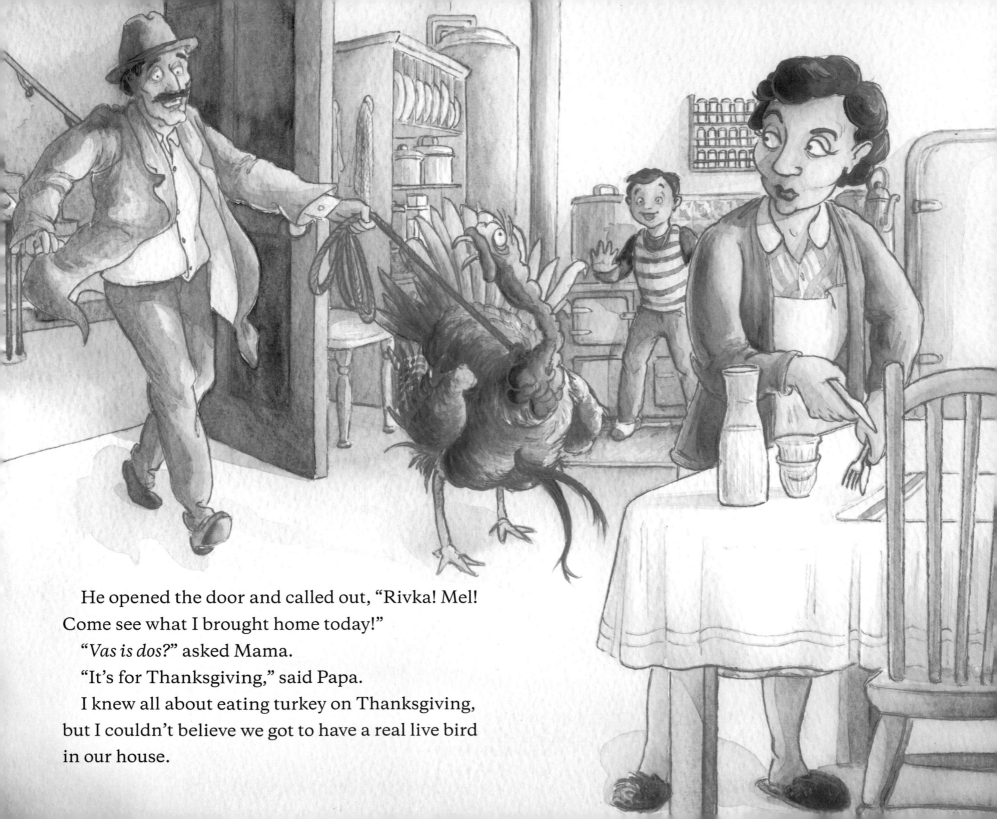

He opened the door and called out, "Rivka! Mel!
Come see what I brought home today!"

"*Vas is dos?*" asked Mama.

"It's for Thanksgiving," said Papa.

I knew all about eating turkey on Thanksgiving,
but I couldn't believe we got to have a real live bird
in our house.

The turkey followed me around the apartment all afternoon, gobble-gobbling.

Papa said the turkey was a *he*. Every time I turned around, the turkey would stick out his tail and puff up his feathers. Papa said that was because the turkey thought I was a hen. That made me laugh.

Papa thought we should call the turkey Indik. That's the Yiddish word for turkey. Mama didn't think we should name the turkey at all.

"A turkey doesn't belong in a fourth-floor walk-up!" said Mama. "He belongs with Mr. Cohen."

Mr. Cohen was our butcher. I didn't want to think about bringing Indik there.

But Mama was thinking about what to make for Thanksgiving, which was in only two days. Now that we had a turkey, she was inviting the whole family to dinner. Aunt Shaindel was making stuffed cabbage and Aunt Hanaleh was bringing her famous noodle kugel.

"Now we'll have turkey too," said Mama. "Just like all the neighbors."

I sat at the window, leaning against Indik's feathers. I didn't want to lose him.

The next morning, Papa said we had to bring Indik over to Mr. Cohen's shop before school.

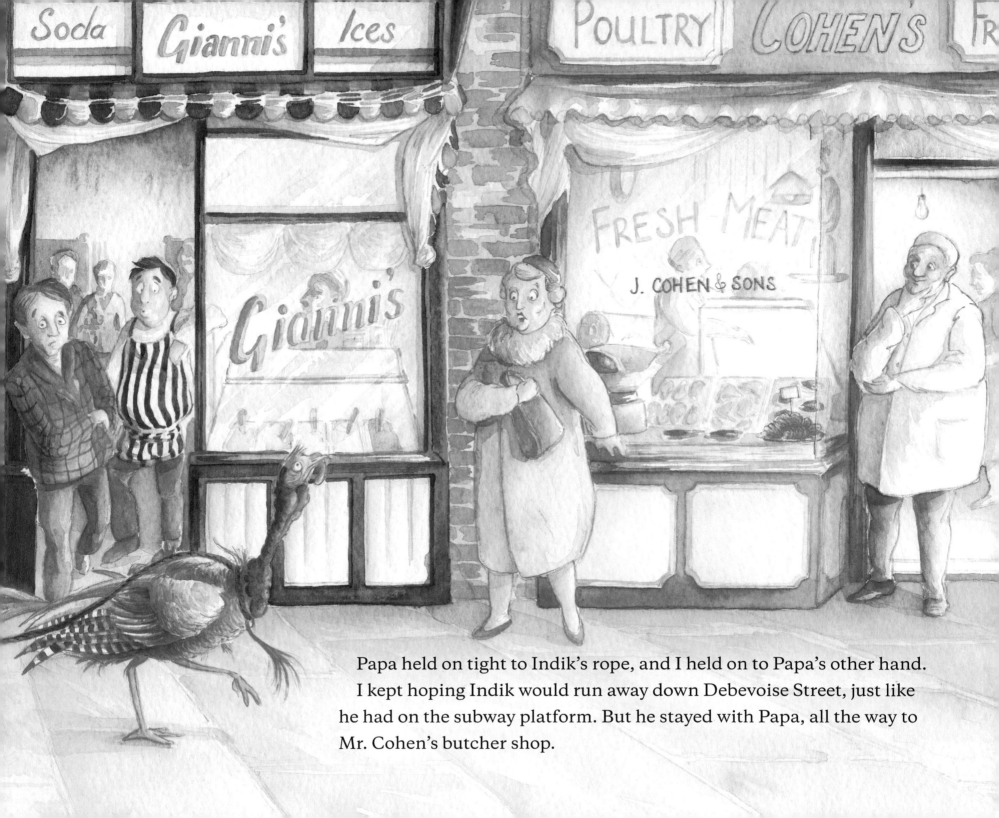

Papa held on tight to Indik's rope, and I held on to Papa's other hand. I kept hoping Indik would run away down Debevoise Street, just like he had on the subway platform. But he stayed with Papa, all the way to Mr. Cohen's butcher shop.

"Where'd you get that bird?" asked Mr. Cohen. "He must weigh at least thirty pounds."

"I won him at the raffle at work," said Papa. "He's for our first Thanksgiving dinner."

I looked at Indik to see if he was listening. I wanted him to know that if we cooked him for dinner, I wasn't going to eat him.

Then I held my breath, waiting to see what Mr. Cohen would say.

"Not this turkey," said Mr. Cohen with a big laugh. "He's too old! He'll be too tough to eat."

What a relief! I thought.

"Let him stay here with me and eat all the scraps in the yard," he said.

"But what will we eat for Thanksgiving dinner?" asked Papa. "Mama already invited the whole family over."

"Stick with the side dishes," said Mr. Cohen. "They're the best part of the holiday."

I ran home after school to tell Mama we wouldn't be having Indik for Thanksgiving dinner.

"But what will we serve?" she asked. "We can't just have kugel and stuffed cabbage. That's not what Americans eat."

"Yes, we can," I told Mama. "Mrs. Caporimo said it's important to serve foods from the old country. She said she's making lasagna. And I bet Mrs. Murphy is making Irish soda bread."

"That's their tradition," said Mama. She stopped to think for a moment. "But I guess it makes sense. It's our first Thanksgiving, so we'll make the foods that feel special to us."

On Thanksgiving Day, Uncle Moshe and Aunt Shaindel, Aunt Hanaleh and Uncle Max, Pearl and Joey, Bluma and Sam all came over.

We sat down at the table, which was really the kitchen table and the sewing machine pushed together and covered with Mama's best white tablecloth.

Mama brought out a big noodle kugel, and Aunt Shaindel carried in the stuffed cabbage.

"Who needs turkey?" said Papa, and we all laughed.

He looked at all of us and said, "This is what we're thankful for—that we're all here and we're all together."

Guess what? Eating noodle kugel on
Thanksgiving became our family's tradition.

And Indik liked it too. I brought him a big
piece the next day and he ate it all up.

# Cranberry Apple Kugel Recipe

Mama and Aunt Hanaleh didn't put cranberries in their noodle kugel, probably because fresh cranberries—or even dried cranberries—were not available in stores when they first moved to America. But here's our recipe for noodle kugel. Adding cranberries gives it the Thanksgiving touch.

## Ingredients

| | |
|---|---|
| 8 oz fresh cranberries | ½ C sugar |
| ¾ C water | 1 tsp fresh lemon zest |
| 2 tsp cornstarch | 1 ½ lbs wide egg noodles (one and a half packages) |
| ½ C margarine or butter | ¾ C sugar |
| 1 tsp cinnamon plus extra | 3 large apples, peeled and thinly sliced |
| 5 large eggs | |

Place cranberries, ½ cup of sugar, water, and lemon zest in a saucepan over medium heat. Wait until water begins to boil, then add cornstarch, and stir. Continue to simmer until cranberries are soft and sauce thickens. Add a little water if needed. Set aside to cool.

Cook noodles in a large pot. Drain well and set aside.

Preheat oven to 350°F degrees and grease a 9" x 13" pan.

Melt margarine or butter, and mix with ¾ cup of sugar, cinnamon, and apples.

Separate eggs and beat egg whites until frothy and thick. Add egg yolks to sugar-apple mixture. Add noodles and mix well. Gently fold egg whites into noodle mixture.

Spread half the noodle mixture into the pan. Add a layer of the cranberry sauce. Add the remaining noodles. Sprinkle with a very light dusting of cinnamon.

Bake 50-55 minutes or until desired crispness on top.